SNIFFING OUT THE KILLER

DOG DETECTIVE - THE BEAGLE MYSTERIES

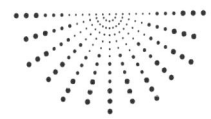

ROSIE SAMS

AGATHA PARKER

SWEETBOOKHUB.COM

THE DOG DETECTIVES – THE BEAGLE MYSTERIES

Welcome to my book. I recently joined forces with the amazing Rosie Sams to work on this wonderful series of cozy mystery books all featuring a sweet little Beagle puppy. Mazie in the books is an ex-police dog who was wounded in service. She is gifted to Hannah Barry, a broken-hearted realtor who is down on her luck.

At first, Hannah is unsure, can she learn to love the Beagle? What will she do when a body is found?

Find out if Mazie has found a new home and if Hannah finds some peace in Sniffing out the killer the first in a fabulous series of cozy mysteries.

Grab free short stories and be the first to find out when Rosie has a new release by joining her free newsletter

CHAPTER ONE

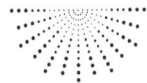

*H*annah looked up at the vibrant colors on the trees lining her street. The cheerful red and rich auburn of the leaves were in direct contrast to her mood. *How can the leaves be so happy when they are about to fall to their death?* She was just one block from her cozy little house where she'd curl up by the fire, drink some cider, and feel sorry for herself. She just had to make it past his house first. It was enough that she lived one block from Peter Royce, her ex-boyfriend. But now she had to pass by his home every single day on her morning walk. She wrapped her scarf up over her nose and tucked her head down into it. Maybe he wouldn't see her.

It was then that she heard the squeal of tires and watched as a little blue sports car took a tight, tidy turn into Peter's driveway. She felt her blood run cold and her feet involuntarily stopped moving. Out of the driver's seat popped a stylish, petite brunette wearing a shade of bright pink lipstick. The foolish man had always preferred brunette's, saying her blonde was a little washed out.

The new woman slipped gracefully up the front steps of the house and there, waiting for her, was Peter. His tall frame filled the doorway, he wrapped the brunette into a tight squeeze and gave her a kiss on the lips. Hannah knew he hadn't been faithful; that's why they'd broken up. But she didn't think she'd have to watch him with his new girlfriend with her very own eyes. She felt acid rise in her throat and hid behind a big oak tree, taking deep breaths in and out. When she heard his front door close, she looked up to the crisp, blue sky.

Oh, you've got a lot of nerve looking bright and beautiful on a day like today. Can't you see that people down here are suffering? If she couldn't yell at Peter, she'd yell at the sky.

Slamming her hand in her pocket she pulled out her phone. Maybe checking on her precious few house listings would distract her. "Ugh, no alerts!" she muttered and toggled over to her bank app to see what her current balance was. More depression and a big gulp. "I guess I'll have to dip into my savings again this month." Pressing her fingers into the tender skin under her eyes she bit down. "I will not cry today. I will not cry today." However, she did need to sell a house. And soon.

When she arrived at her own cozy little place a smile came to her lips. Colorful potted plants lining the front porch and filling her with joy, she felt her shoulders relax. It was time for that cider. But when she walked up the steps to her door, she was startled by a deep voice.

"Hey cuz! Did you forget we were meeting today?"

Hannah jumped as if an armed thug had just accosted her, throwing her hand to her heart to steady the erratic beating. "Ahhh!" she shrieked, momentarily startled out of her self-pity. Then the familiar curly blond hair of her cousin finally registered. "Niles! Oh, I'm so sorry. I did completely space out our meeting today. But it's so nice to see a familiar face." She let herself sink into the empty spot beside him on the porch swing.

Niles' long legs stretched to the railing. His easy grin turned up at the corners of his mouth. "Well, did you at least remember that I was bringing a surprise for you?"

Hannah lifted her brows in anticipation. "My favorite donuts? This is the perfect day for some of those."

Niles shook his head.

"A macchiato? That would also be a lovely treat."

His grin got wider, but he shook his head again.

"Fine, I give up." She crossed her legs under her body and turned to face Niles.

"I know you've been going through a tough time lately. And I really want to help make you feel better about things."

Despite herself, Hannah felt the well of tears forming. Swallowing, she strained her eyes and willed them not to fall.

"I wish I could be here more to help out, but as I can't... I've arranged for a proxy."

Hannah looked into Niles' deep blue eyes, searching for something to help her understand.

He stood up, stretching to his full height, his head ducking his six-foot frame to avoid a hanging plant. "Close your eyes."

Hannah obediently placed her hands over her face. "This better be good."

She heard the shuffle of Niles' feet across the wood beams of her porch move away from her, and then come back. Then she felt the warm, wet slide of something move up her cheek. "What in the world?" she lurched back in her seat, dropping her hands from her face.

OMG, sitting proudly on the porch swing and staring at her with big, brown eyes shining playfully, was a... dog. It looked at Hannah. Waiting.

Hannah released a nervous chuckle and turned to Niles. "Heh, heh. Good one! Is this your way of cheering me up, by joking about getting me a puppy?" She placed her hands on her lap and gave the dog a sideways glance. It was still staring at her.

"Actually," Niles said. "She's not a puppy. She's three years old, and her name is Mazie.

Hannah looked at the tricolored dog with floppy ears and a long tail. "So, is it a bulldog?"

Niles laughed. "Not a dog person, are you? This is a beagle. They are some of the most loyal, lovable, and intelligent dogs you will ever come across. And this little sweetie is also one of the bravest dogs you'll ever know.

She was shot in the line of duty and saved someone's life in the process." Niles scratched behind Mazie's ears, causing her tail to flop cheerfully against the cushion.

An unconscious smile began to form on one side of Hannah's mouth. "Cute. Mazie, you're a cutie." Then she looked at Niles. "Well, it worked, she cheered me up. Thanks for the surprise. Should we head inside to warm up?" She lifted herself from the swing.

"Well, that was easier than I thought it would be. So, you'll take her?" Niles asked.

Hannah spun around to face him. *"Take her?* What do you mean, I thought you just brought her by for a visit?"

Niles' face fell slightly, realizing the miscommunication. "Hannah, I brought Mazie here for you as a gift. *She's* the surprise. She needs a loving home since her injury, and you... well," Niles scratched the back of his neck. "I thought maybe you could use some, er, company." His cheeks flushed slightly as he looked at Hannah.

Hannah's blue eyes went so wide she thought they might pop out of her head and she released a tiny squeak. "Gift? You want me to take Mazie... a dog?" She tilted her head and waited for his response.

As if on cue, Mazie jumped off of the porch swing, walked to Hannah's legs, and rubbed her snout against Hannah's legs before sitting proudly beside her.

Hannah felt something inside of her warm. She noted Mazie's wagging tail. *Mazie is more cheerful than the blue sky. She's ridiculously happy after having been shot. It was like Mazie didn't even remember it happened.*

Niles noticed the way Hannah looked at the dog and went in for the kill. "Look, why don't you just take her for a trial period. If things don't work out, you can give the lovely little Mazie back, no questions asked."

Hannah didn't object, so Niles continued. "Two weeks. Call it an experiment. Call it babysitting. Call it a sleepover! Whatever you want to call it, there's no pressure."

"Okay. Fine. Two weeks." Hannah's eyes met Niles'.

"Yeah! This is going to be great! You won't regret it. Mazie is the best, you two will be an amazing team."

Hannah reached down to pet Mazie.

"I need to get to work. Crime doesn't stop for any dog, right, Mazie?" Niles waved goodbye and headed to his shift as a state police officer. Hannah watched him leave with a mixture of pride; what a great guy her cousin was, and annoyance; what had her great cousin just gotten her into?

Hannah opened the door and Mazie obediently followed her inside. She crouched down and locked eyes with the dog. "A great team, huh? I wonder what sort of trouble you are going to get into?"

Mazie wagged her tail furiously, overjoyed to be with her new owner.

Hannah couldn't help but note Mazie's resilience, and despite herself, she found a smile crossing her own face.

CHAPTER TWO

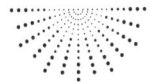

The next morning Hannah woke to a giant sloppy lick up the side of her face. Disoriented, she sat straight up, looking for the source of the warm, rough sensation. When she saw Mazie, she lurched away, forgetting in her sleepiness that she'd agreed to host a dog for two weeks. She scooted so far back that she rolled off the bed, landing with a thunk on the floor. "Ow!" She rubbed her backside.

Mazie wasted no time and leaped to the floor, licking Hannah's face in rapid succession as she wiggled and snuffled all over her.

Despite wanting to be grumpy, Hannah began to giggle. "Right. Morning, Mazie," she rubbed the back of Mazie's soft head and looked up at the clock. "8:30! I was supposed to be up forty-five minutes ago, I've got a showing for Priscilla Bryant!"

Hannah jumped to her feet and ran to the bathroom to splash water on her face. She brushed her teeth and ran a comb through her hair then sprayed it with some dry shampoo. Pulling on some clothes she nipped back to the mirror to swipe a quick wipe of mascara over her lashes, pinched her cheeks, and dabbed some clear gloss on her lips. "This will have to do," she said to her reflection.

Mazie was underfoot the whole time, keeping pace with Hannah's quick steps around the house. As she hustled to the kitchen, Mazie raced in front of her causing Hannah to stumble slightly. "Mazie! Sit. I have to get going." Mazie sat, but her body wiggled, itching to move as her big brown eyes followed Hannah around the room. Hannah grabbed a bagel and stuffed it in her purse. "I won't be long, Mazie! Be a good girl."

As Hannah approached the front door, Mazie began to whine. "Awe, don't be sad." She glanced in the bag Niles had brought over yesterday and reached in to find a chew toy. She tossed it over to Mazie. "This should keep you occupied."

Mazie watched the toy sail through the air and land beside her. She looked at the toy and ignored it, staring back at Hannah with her sad, puppy-dog eyes.

Hannah felt a twitch in her heart, the same one she experienced yesterday when deciding to let Mazie stay. "Ugh, okay! You can come!" She grabbed the harness and leash from the bag and secured Mazie.

The little dog's tail wagged so vigorously that her little bottom was swaying right along with it. Opening the door she checked her watch. "Okay Mazie, walk quickly. We have exactly 7 minutes to get there. And Mrs. Bryant does not like it when people are late." She and Mazie scampered down her driveway to the sidewalk and in the direction of Priscilla Bryant's house.

At 9:00 on the dot, Hannah and Mazie rang the doorbell of Priscilla Bryant. Hannah couldn't help but calculate the potential commission of the beautiful home. This sale would certainly get her back on track. She heard the clip of heels approach, and a woman with dark eyes rimmed with a harsh black liner opened the door, blasting Hannah with her woodsy perfume.

"Hello! Mrs. Bryant. Thank you for the opportunity to show your home today. I have a good feeling about the couple stopping by." Hannah took in Priscilla's perfectly coiffed hair and silk shirt, trying not to be intimidated.

Priscilla looked Hannah up and down, taking in her slightly wrinkled blouse, and black pants with traces of fur stuck to them. Then her eyes trailed to Mazie. Her brows lifted and she looked to Hannah for an explanation.

"Oh," Hannah blushed. "This is Mazie. She'll be no trouble at all."

Priscilla looked at her watch. "Well, there's no time for debate." With a lift of her perfect brows, she widened the door for them to enter. "And you'll remember, of course, that this isn't my home. It belonged to my late brother, Willard."

"Of course. I'm so sorry for your loss."

"Hopefully, you will help make up for my loss with a profit on the home," Priscilla replied.

Hannah gulped as she followed behind Priscilla. She couldn't see her face to know if she was kidding or not, so she stayed silent. But she found herself inexplicably turning to Mazie as if to share in a *what in the world?* moment. Mazie just wagged her tail.

"Willard died in a tragic fishing accident. I was always left to clean up his messes, even when we were children. I suppose this is a fitting end for us both. But you'll make a profit for me, and it will be the least I deserve, after all I've done for Willard."

Hannah had no idea how to respond, so chose to shift the conversation back to the house. "You won't be disappointed. I've been putting all of my efforts into your, I mean, your late brother's home, and believe I've found a couple who are very interested. They are going to join me here soon," Hannah hinted to Priscilla, hoping she'd excuse herself. It was frowned upon for the owner to be there during a showing, it tended to make the buyers uncomfortable.

Priscilla either did not get the hint or chose to ignore it and sat down on a stool at the counter. Then the doorbell rang.

Mazie began barking and ran to the front door. Hannah's face flushed. "That must be the Weavers." She rushed to the front door, shushing Mazie along the way. "Megan and Tom! Thank you so much for coming to view this lovely home today," gushed Hannah.

"Nice to meet you," Tom said, shaking Hannah's hand. Megan did the same. Mazie sniffed their feet, causing them to step over her. "I didn't realize the house had a dog," Megan said, her button of a nose a little in the air.

Hannah forced her smile even wider but did not confirm or deny Megan's assumption. "This is Mazie," she said simply.

The Weavers were a smart looking couple in their mid-20's with brown hair and pale faces. They were both around 5 foot eight and if she hadn't known better she would have thought them, brother and sister. They removed their polished black shoes and made their way into the kitchen where they saw Priscilla waiting.

"This is Priscilla Bryant, the seller," offered Hannah awkwardly.

"Oh," startled Megan. "How unconventional. I'm a realtor myself and this isn't very common, is it?" she looked to her husband.

"Not common at all," Tom forced a strained smile.

"Hm," was all Priscilla said as she looked at the young couple. "I'll be on the porch, then." With a toss of her hair, she walked by them to sit outside.

Hannah breathed a sigh of relief. "Let's continue the tour then, shall we?"

Megan dropped her purse on the counter and followed behind Hannah. They walked around the house, discussing the incredible school district, how the street was filled with other young families, and how safe the neighborhood was. The Weavers complimented everything from the cabinet colors to the size of the bedrooms, and Hannah was feeling confident about the sale.

Mazie faithfully followed the group as they toured the home, her sharp hound's nose leaving no corner unsniffed. About halfway through the tour, Mazie dropped away. The other three were so focused on the details of the home, they didn't notice.

Hannah passed a door near the kitchen and began to turn the handle. "This will be the basement, probably not too exciting."

"I think we've seen enough to have made our decision," Tom said.

Hannah took her hand off the knob and led the Weavers back to the kitchen, ending the tour. When they arrived, they found that Mazie had hopped up on a stool with her front paws on the counter, and was sniffing Megan's purse. She had pushed the purse to the edge so that it was dangling off.

"Mazie!" Hannah yelled. "I'm so sorry about this," she tried.

Megan grabbed her purse and clutched it tightly to her chest. "This has been one of the least professional showings I've ever been to," she fumed. "First, the owner is here, and now the dog!"

Hannah could feel the sale slipping between her fingers and quickly clipped Mazie's leash onto her harness. "I can't apologize enough. I assure you that this is not a typical showing for me. Please, accept my sincere regret."

Megan and Tom stepped to the side and whispered to one another for a few minutes. When they separated, Megan looked at Hannah. "Despite the hiccups today, we do love the home, and would like to make an offer."

Hannah took in a slow breath and held it, waiting to hear the price. When Megan said the number, Hannah had to tell herself not to show her disappointment. "That's quite a bit below asking," she said carefully.

Before Megan or Tom could say anything in response, a screeching voice rang out from the porch. "That's not just below asking, that's an insult, it's highway robbery! I'd rather sell my brother himself for that amount of money! I wouldn't even be able to pay for his funeral bills for what you are offering!"

Hannah's eyes went wide. Mazie sensed the tension and raced to the porch, barking in the direction of Priscilla.

Megan stiffened. She grabbed Tom's arm and began to steer them to the door. "This has been a disgrace. The dog, the owner, and now this... scene! Hannah, I'll be filing a complaint with your firm."

Now it was Hannah's turn to tense up. She could not afford to lose this sale, and she definitely could not afford a complaint with her firm! "Mrs. Weaver, please. Let's discuss this further. Remember the cabinets you love? And what about the size of those rooms!" her voice carried behind them as they stomped to the exit. Mazie sniffed them again as they put their shoes back on. When Megan's purse dropped off of her arm, Mazie shoved her nose in it, digging around as though it contained a freshly cooked chicken.

"Mazie! Leave it!" Hannah scolded, mortified.

Megan angrily handed Tom her purse to hold as she finished putting on her shoes. Hannah noticed that her face was a deep scarlet. Megan shoved Mazie away with her hand, causing her to slide across the hardwood floors toward Hannah. Though Hannah was humiliated and upset with Mazie herself, that gesture startled her. But she had to be careful as they were still potential buyers. "Shall we try the tour again? Maybe tomorrow? No owners, no dogs?"

Tom helped Megan back to standing. "I think we need some time to process. Thanks, Hannah. We'll be in touch." At this, he held the door open for his wife, holding her arm as they walked down the steps to their car, ignoring Priscilla's 'tsking' as they passed.

When the Weavers were in their car, Mazie ran to the kitchen, then back to Hannah, nudging her legs. Hannah didn't notice, as she was more focused on Priscilla's scowl. Mazie ran back to the kitchen and returned to sniffing the perimeter of the room.

"You call that an offer? You call those potential buyers?" Priscilla's voice increased with each word. "I call that a JOKE!"

"I understand, Mrs. Bryant. That was not a typical situation, I..."

Priscilla cut her off, "You have one week to sell this place, or I'm finding new representation!"

Hannah's face flushed, and she could feel her body warm. Nodding, she walked to the front door. "I won't let you down, Mrs. Bryant." Hannah felt like she was forgetting something but was so distracted by the nightmare of a showing, she couldn't think clearly enough to put her finger on what it was. Then she heard pawing and scratching. *Mazie!*

Mazie was sniffing and whining at the door by the kitchen. Hannah looked on curiously. They hadn't gone in there on the tour. It must be the pantry.

Priscilla's voice broke through her thoughts. "Take your mutt and leave!" she scolded. Hannah startled to action and rushed over to grab the leash still attached and dragging behind Mazie.

"Let's go, Mazie," Hannah whispered, a bead of sweat forming on her upper lip.

"I won't let you down!" was all she could think to say when she called back to Mrs. Bryant.

Once they were a safe distance away from the house, Hannah looked at Mazie. "You just ruined my chance of a sale! Don't you know how much I needed this today?" She knew Mazie couldn't understand her, but Hannah could swear she saw the little dog's head drop and knew she was upset as they moved along the sidewalk.

Hannah focused her eyes ahead of her and stomped back to her own house. She tried to make sense of the disaster that had just transpired, playing it back to see how it had all gone so wrong. Her mind paused at the image of Mazie sniffing at the door in the kitchen, as she was trying to leave. What could she have been smelling behind it?

CHAPTER THREE

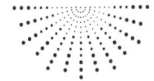

Once Hannah was back home, she poured food and water for Mazie, hoping it would keep the dog occupied while she sat down at her desk to figure out how to fix the mess that had just been made. Hannah scrolled through her contacts to see if any others who'd walked through the recent open house would be potential buyers. She flipped through her files, reading her notes about each visitor who'd come through. She sent a few follow-up emails out and slumped back in her chair. Mazie had finished eating and had curled up beside her on the floor, her nose just resting on Hannah's bare foot. Hannah couldn't help but feel comforted by the soft nuzzle. She sighed. The offer from the Weavers *was* laughably low, but something about Priscilla's response felt... off. Why had she been so... almost violent... in her refusal?

Hannah repositioned herself at her computer and opened up a new search bar. She carefully typed in the name *Priscilla Bryant*. Perhaps she could discover a social media profile, maybe an old high school yearbook photo, but what popped up blew her away. Dozens of photos of Priscilla walking out of a courthouse populated the top line. Below them were links to articles all with the same theme; *Priscilla Bryant Loses Copyright Case*. Hannah clicked on the first link. The article detailed a years-long battle between Priscilla's string of boutique clothing stores, and her competitor, who had sued her for a substantial amount of money claiming she had breached their copyright.

Priscilla owned seven successful boutique clothing stores across Manhattan and had – according to the article – sold and manufactured a purse that looked mysteriously like a very popular one the plaintiff created years before. What's more, just last month the judge had ruled on the case. And it was not in Priscilla's favor. No wonder she had been so staunch about getting the asking price for her brother's home. This would be the only way she could pay what she now owed from the lawsuit! Hannah's jaw dropped slightly when she read the amount of the damages owed. The sale of her brother's house would barely cover them all.

Hannah shifted in her seat, then stood up. She began pacing around her kitchen. Stopping at the coffee machine, she poured herself another cup. She needed to think clearly. Mazie stood up and followed Hannah, keeping tight to her heels. Priscilla's brother had just died. Of a sudden and tragic fishing accident, no less. What were the chances that her brother would pass away, leaving his big house to his sister, at this exact time? Could the violent response she had to the low-ball offer from the Weavers be about more than the house itself? Which was a polite way to say... *might* her brother's death have been more than an accident? And worse, could Priscilla have been responsible for it? Hannah's brain was turning as she cupped her mug of coffee, carefully pacing back and forth, her budding theory making more sense with each sip she took.

Mazie was on alert, sensing Hannah's energy. When Hannah stopped pacing to sip her coffee, Mazie whined, and ran to the front door. Hannah was so deep in thought she wasn't even bothered by the disruption; she could use some fresh air to reflect on her new realization. Grabbing the leash, she clipped it on Mazie, opening the door to let them both walk off the stress.

CHAPTER FOUR

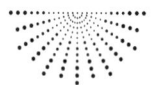

Hannah's mind raced as she walked down the street. She was so distracted she wasn't bothered by Mazie's constant pulling on the leash. The little dog was having a whale of a time sniffing for squirrels and other scents her hound's nose picked up. Instinctively, Hannah made her way in the direction of her favorite coffee shop: Jolt of Java. Not because she needed more caffeine in her body, but because two of her best friends, Oscar and Anita Gomez, owned the coffee shop, and she needed to run her theory past someone.

When she and Mazie arrived at the storefront, Hannah felt herself relax just looking through the window at the rich wood accents and the glazed pine tables. Drifting towards her was the distinct burnt-bean smell of coffee roasting. She and Mazie both inhaled a big sniff as they approached the door.

Oscar looked up from behind the counter and saw Hannah at the door with Mazie. Hannah felt better just looking at them. The two were always so friendly, with their olive skin and brown hair and big understanding brown eyes they just always made her feel better.

Oscar touched his wife's arm and pointed. "This must be the famous dog we've heard so much about!"

They both removed their aprons, leaving the counter under the control of their teenaged barista. They walked to meet Hannah at the door, greeting her with a hug.

"Why don't you and Anita catch up a little bit," Oscar said giving her an understanding smile. "That way, I can stay out here and spend time with this little angel." Oscar leaned down to scratch Mazie behind her ears. Her tail wagged ferociously.

Hannah eyed Mazie's tail and couldn't help but chuckle. "It does look like you two will get along just fine."

Oscar's face was right up against Mazie's nuzzling her as he made little coochy noises.

Hannah watched the two of them with amusement. "In fact, why don't you take Mazie when Niles returns. Then I won't have to be responsible for the little mutt anymore."

Anita frowned at Hannah, surprised at the way she referenced the adorable dog. "It seems to me like the two of you are getting along like two peas in a pod, why would you want to give her up?"

Hannah corrected herself. "You're right. She's not a mutt. She's actually a very beautiful beagle, who's incredibly intelligent and also very soft and brave," she bent down to pet the little dog. "But she's also a lot of work and she may have cost me a sale."

Anita nodded, then carefully continued. "I wonder, do you think you could be shying away from committing fully to Mazie because you are a little nervous about opening yourself up to companionship again, after..." her voice lowered, "Peter?"

Hannah's head jerked to look at Anita. "What? How are the two even remotely related?"

Anita stayed quiet, letting Hannah process.

"Peter wasn't a dog. He was my boyfriend. I didn't have to feed Peter and take him for walks. We were a couple. Closing my heart to Mazie has nothing to do with me closing my heart to Peter." As the words came out of her mouth, she began to understand what Anita might have been referencing. But she wasn't about to admit it.

"You're right, Peter was not a pet. But I do think there is something to be said for allowing yourself to feel love and companionship again."

Hannah opened her mouth to respond but was interrupted by a call on her phone. She jumped at the chance to exit the conversation. "Hello, Hannah Barry speaking." She turned her back to Anita and took a few steps away to gain some privacy.

"Ms. Barry! How are you?" A rich baritone voice rang through the receiver.

Hannah recognized it immediately. It was a developer from Manhattan who called occasionally, though they'd never got as far as a sale. This could be a very good thing. "Mr. Troughton, it's so lovely to hear from you again." Her face flushed with hope, and if she was honest, a little something else as well. Colin Troughton was tall and handsome with a thick head of immaculately styled dark hair, and an equally well-groomed beard. His piercing green eyes stood in stark contrast to his dark hair and skin, almost popping out at you when you spoke with him.

"Always lovely to speak with you, Ms. Barry."

Hannah was glad he wasn't there to see her beam. "What can I do for you today?"

"I received your email this morning and want to see the Bryant property. As soon as possible."

Hannah suppressed the excitement that filled her chest. She leveled her voice. "I'd be happy to show you the property. I think it would serve your purposes well."

"Great, I'll get on a flight tomorrow then."

"Mr. Troughton, before you make arrangements, we should clarify something. The seller is very firm on the asking price. I need to know what sort of offer you are intending to extend before you come all the way here and potentially waste your time." *And mine*, she thought.

"I've been watching this property for years. I'll do whatever it takes to sweeten the deal to make the property mine. You tell me what needs to happen, I'll make it happen."

Hannah smiled from ear to ear. This could be the solution to her little bank account issue, and Priscilla's legal issues. She hoped Colin couldn't hear her eagerness over the phone. "I'll arrange a viewing for tomorrow then. And I'll have the papers ready to go."

"My assistant is booking a flight now. I'll see you tomorrow at 10am."

And within those two minutes, everything was looking up for Hannah. She turned to face Anita and Oscar. They were both fawning all over Mazie, treating the little dog as though she was their first-born baby. She couldn't let anything mess up this deal. It was too good to be true, and if Mazie came near the Bryant house again, Hannah wasn't confident it would be a sure thing. "So, Oscar. What do you think about spending some more time with Mazie over the next day or two?"

Without hesitation, Oscar agreed. "Say no more, Hannah. This dog will brighten anyone's day. You don't have to ask me twice to spend more time with her."

Hannah felt her body relax with relief. Then she met Mazie's brown eyes, looking up at her inquisitively and something switched. "Don't worry, Mazie. It's just for two days. I'll be back before you know it."

At this, Anita cleared her throat. Hannah knew she was nearing *I told you* so territory and refused to meet her eyes. Instead, she threw her arms around both Anita and Oscar. "You are the best. I'll be back for her tomorrow!" and she turned away. Walking to get the paperwork started.

CHAPTER FIVE

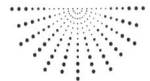

*H*annah woke up the next morning to her alarm, not dog licks. She sat up in bed with a sense of purpose and optimism for the day. Today will change the direction of everything. Colin is coming to town and he's got deep pockets. He'll buy the house; I'll pay my bills and my luck will begin again.

At 9:50 A.M. Hannah was at the Bryant home making sure every detail was in place before Colin arrived. She moved lamps an inch to the left, straightened cushions, and wiped her palm across various surfaces. If the already pristine house had a hint of dust before, it wouldn't stand a chance against Hannah's attention to detail.

The doorbell sounded at exactly 10:00 A.M. Hannah was at the door, hand on the doorknob. She swung it open and was met with a pair of dazzling green eyes. The contrast of their green against Colin's olive skin made Hannah's skin tingle. *Seal the deal,* she scolded herself, nothing more.

"Hannah," he greeted her with his smooth voice. He reached toward her, gently placed his hands on her shoulders, and gave each of her cheeks a kiss.

An involuntary blush came to her cheeks. She was always professional, but his greeting was very Manhattan compared to the usual firm handshake of Blairstown. Taken aback by the heat from his nearness, she managed to recover with a voice slightly higher than her usual octave. "Mr. Troughton, welcome to Blairstown." She smiled and scooted her body back in an attempt to provide some distance between them.

"Call me Colin, please," he insisted. His eyes cast down at her as he smoothed his custom suit. Hannah noted his confident stride as he walked through the front foyer to the kitchen in a way that made it seem as though he already owned the home.

"Hi, Colin. Of course. It's so gracious of you to make the trip at such short notice. Thank you for coming so soon."

He picked up a trinket on the kitchen shelf and placed it back down dismissively, as though it would be the first thing to go when he bought the property "No bother, it's what I do. Shall we?" He gestured to the upstairs, requesting to see the rest of the home.

"Of course, follow me." Hannah scurried ahead of him, leading him through the house tour. As they toured Colin left no space un-seen, Hannah managed to muster the courage to ask him about the asking price again. She cleared her throat. "So, Colin. You mentioned on the phone that the asking price seemed reasonable to you." She paused, letting the statement hang awkwardly in the air.

Colin peaked in a closet, moving clothes out of the way to see every corner. "I'll offer you exactly what you are asking."

Colin's back was to her, so Hannah took the opportunity to close her fist and bring her elbow tight to her sides, *yes!* she mimed to herself. Just as quickly, she relaxed her arm and feigned nonchalance as best she could. "Wonderful. That sounds wonderful," she said. "I've got the paperwork in the kitchen." She hoped she was keeping the desperation out of her voice.

Colin clasped his hands together and let his eyes rest on Hannah a beat longer than necessary before responding. "I've seen all I need to see," his face slid into a sly smile. "Let's sign those papers."

Hannah turned quickly away from Colin so he wouldn't see the effect he had on her and walked briskly to the kitchen. "Here you go, just sign here and here," she said, pointing to the pre-tabbed signature lines.

Colin signed the papers and Hannah produced a set of keys from her purse. "Here you are. Congratulations on your new home!" Hannah reached out to shake his hand.

The palm of his hand met hers in a firm shake, then he gently slid his other hand to hold her extended wrist. It was a warm gesture, indicating a partnership that was familiar, but Hannah felt the intimacy of his touch spark her skin. "I, I'll... I'll be in touch later today, possibly tomorrow," she stuttered.

Colin released a self-assured smile. "Why don't we make it sooner than that. I'll take you to dinner tonight." It didn't sound like a question as much as a given.

Hannah's eyes widened. "Coffee?" she blurted. This man was undoubtedly attractive, but he had a way of knocking her off-kilter. "I know a spot just down the road." She wanted to get him to Jolt of Java where she'd have the support of Oscar and Anita.

Colin seemed all-too-eager to accept. "I'll see you there, just tell me a time."

Hannah glanced at her watch and suggested they meet in an hour so she could finish everything up. He agreed and left. Relieved, Hannah reached for her phone to call Priscilla with the great news. "Mrs. Bryant, you'll be pleased to hear that we have a confirmed buyer! He's signed the paperwork already. Once you sign the papers, you've officially sold your home! Call me and we can discuss the details. I handed over a set of keys as per the instructions on file." Hannah felt relief wash through her body. Nothing could ruin this day.

An hour later, Hannah had wrapped up her paperwork. Despite her nagging feeling about Colin being a little bit too smug for her taste, she headed to the coffee shop. She'd be there with Oscar and Anita, after all. She would be interested to hear their opinion. They were almost always right about people, having the knack to see through the veneer to the real person beneath. Hannah had an extra pep in her step, she didn't know if it was because she had sold the house, or because she was meeting Colin. Or because she was going to see Mazie again. *That can't be it,* she thought to herself.

But when she arrived at Jolt of Java, she saw Colin's muscular silhouette in the window sitting at a table waiting for her. And she saw Oscar at the door, holding Mazie's leash with the excited pup watching Hannah carefully, wagging her tail. *She can't recognize me already,* Hannah thought. But sure enough, when she got closer Mazie scampered over to Hannah who crouched down, and Mazie licked her face. Hannah squealed at the joy of someone being so excited to see her and rubbed the little beagle's belly when she rolled over for it. That was when she saw the scar and realized just how badly the dog had been injured and yet she was always happy. Always looking for the good. Maybe she could learn a thing or two from the dog!

"So, who's this cutie?" rang a voice from above.

Hannah looked up to see the piercing green eyes that belonged to Colin.

She flushed slightly, unsure if he was talking about her or Mazie. Hannah stood, flustered, and introduced Colin to Oscar, Anita, and Mazie. Colin smoothed over any awkwardness with his charm and his smile and soon they were all sitting together at a table. Colin carried the conversation, careful to ask Anita and Oscar questions about themselves and compliment the store. All the while, he slipped Mazie tiny pieces of his croissant. The man had everyone close to Hannah eating, sometimes literally, out of the palm of his hand. *Maybe I was wrong about him*, thought Hannah, as she allowed herself to swim in the wake of his charm, along with everyone else.

The magic haze of the moment was unceremoniously interrupted by Hannah's cell phone. She had left the ringer on in case anyone needed her — this deal couldn't suffer any loose ends.

"Hannah Barry here," she answered the phone, turning away from the table slightly. Even if someone had warned her that the call would be shocking, she could not have prepared herself for what was to come. "No! That can't be. Yes, I understand. I'm heading there immediately. Goodbye." She hung up and turned to her friends, slack-jawed.

They were all staring at her, having heard the shock in her voice. "So?" Anita asked, willing her to explain.

Hannah scraped her chair back and stood abruptly. "I've got to get back to the Bryant house." She looked around the table. "That was Kate Carver, the police chief. She has declared the home a crime scene!" Hannah ran toward her car. When she got to the parking spot a few short strides later, she realized that Colin and Mazie were both hot on her trail. "Ugh," she said, exasperated. "Get in, the both of you!" And the three of them climbed in and headed back to the house.

CHAPTER SIX

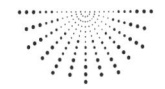

Hannah was careful to keep her wits about her as she drove the tree-lined residential streets back to the house, but she was definitely going above the speed limit. When she arrived, she parked hastily on the street and sprinted up the lawn, Mazie following behind her, leash dragging. Colin was not far behind.

Kate Carver, the local Chief of Police, was waiting for Hannah and walked toward her, a concerned look on her face. Kate knew Hannah well because of her cousin. She was good at her job and fair and young for the position. In her late 30's she was short and slim with a chestnut bob and hazel eyes.

"What in the world is going on?" Hannah asked.

Then Hannah heard a commotion from the house. It was Priscilla Bryant screaming at the police officers in the house, telling them they had no right to be there.

Kate put up her hands as if to stop Hannah from coming any further. "Hannah, the cleaning service you hired to get the house ready for the new owner found blood in the basement."

Hannah gasped and looked over to Colin. Colin stood to his full, imposing height and squared his shoulders for whatever was to come next. Then, she looked at Mazie. Hadn't she been sniffing at a door when she was at the disaster of a showing to the Weavers? Could that have led to the basement? Her mind churned with possibilities. Did Priscilla know about the blood, and was she perhaps panicked that the Weavers would buy the home and find it before she had time to clean it all up? Could that be why she was so bizarrely furious about the low offer?

Kate noticed Hannah go quiet and asked what was on her mind. She stepped toward Kate and pulled her away from Colin slightly. "She was here with me for a showing," she said, gesturing to Mazie. "Mazie was very interested in what was happening down in the basement, but we never went down there on the tour. I just thought she was being a nuisance."

She looked down at Mazie and whispered, "Sorry."

"Interesting, I've heard a lot about Mazie, she has an incredible nose and is a real hero.

Hannah stared at the dog a moment longer before she turned back to Kate. "Priscilla was so angry about the low offer from the couple. At the time I thought she was upset because she had bills to pay, but now I'm wondering if it's because she was worried, she hadn't cleaned up the crime scene!"

Kate nodded. "I think you might be on to something." She looked at the house toward Priscilla. "Please, excuse me." Within moments, Kate had a whispered conversation with one of the officers, and Priscilla was being cuffed and placed in the back of a police car.

Hannah didn't know what to think. She kept twirling her blonde hair around her index finger as she watched the scene around her.

Colin was watching as well, enthralled. "This probably isn't an appropriate time, but... is this going to affect my purchase?" he asked.

Hannah swiveled to look at him. Her face was a rich red, but this time not because she was embarrassed. "Are you really asking me about the state of our deal at a time like this?" she asked, appalled.

Colin placed his hands in his front pockets. "It's a natural question," he shrugged.

"And you are still interested in the home, given there's a bloody crime scene in the basement?" she asked, her voice rising.

"As I mentioned on the phone, I've been watching this property for months. I'm looking out for my best interests. I'm a developer, after all. I don't think that's an odd line of questioning from your client."

Hannah didn't know what to say. But she did know that it felt strange. This wasn't just Colin being smug, this felt like something else. She just couldn't put her finger on what it could be. Any afterglow from their fun coffee with the Gómezes had just worn away.

As if sensing her shift in mood, Mazie began sniffing Colin's expensive leather loafers, and Hannah was sure she heard a low growl. Now Hannah was on alert. After all, Mazie wasn't wrong about the basement. Could it be that Colin had something to do with the death of

Willard Bryant? His nonchalance about buying a home that was an active crime scene did not bode well for her opinion of him. Could it be that his eagerness to close the deal, at full price no less, had something to do with Colin being part of Willard's demise?

CHAPTER SEVEN

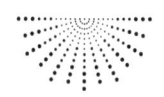

After a long day that began with such high hopes, only to be dashed so dramatically — by a crime scene no less, Hannah sank into bed. Mazie had found her way onto Hannah's bed, and they fell fast asleep together. The next day, Hannah was going to meet Colin at his hotel to discuss the sale. She needed time and space to clear her head and make sense of all that had just happened.

The following morning Hannah got up and fed and walked Mazie finding herself talking to the little dog. Occasionally, she noticed that she limped a little on her right hind leg, the one with the scar. Despite this, her tail never stopped wagging and she would look at Hannah with the most expressive eyes she had ever fallen into.

Hannah was feeling charitable toward Mazie since the dog had provided her comfort from a hard day, so she decided to bring her along on the day's appointments. A little later she entered the lobby of the hotel with Mazie trotting along beside her. She saw the police chief sitting at a table in the restaurant. "Kate, what are you doing here?" she asked.

Kate looked up from her coffee. "Hannah! Believe it or not, this place serves the best brunch in town. What about you?"

"I'm here to talk to Colin Troughton about the Bryant house. We were this close to closing on it yesterday," Hannah held her index finger and thumb an inch apart. "We have a few things to work through now since..." she left the end of the sentence hanging.

"Since the revelation. I see," Kate responded. "Speaking of the revelation; I thought you might be interested to hear that Priscilla Bryant has been protesting — loudly, I should mention — that she has nothing to do with the blood and her brother's death. Can you believe that?" she asked.

Hannah raised her eyebrows. Then she looked around the lobby as if to consider something. "Speaking of

Priscilla, do you mind if I have a seat for a few minutes? I have a few things to run by you."

Kate smiled knowingly. "I hope they're not theories. You realize you should leave the detective work to, you know, the detectives," Kate had a twinkle in her eye, betraying the fondness she had for Hannah, but her voice had a warning edge to it.

"I know, and I understand. I just think you should hear me out on this."

Kate crossed her arms over her chest and sat back in her chair. Hannah took this as an invitation to continue. "Listen, there might be something to Priscilla's objections. I'm not saying she's a good person or even a nice one, but I might have another theory."

Kate couldn't help herself. "Continue."

Hannah looked at her watch. As if on cue, Colin's rich voice rang through the lobby. "Hannah!" he called out. "Hope you aren't eating anything. Our reservation awaits, shall we?" he offered her his elbow as if she was going to hook her arm into his. She waved it away with her hand. "Hi, Colin. I'll be right there, I'm just finishing up with my friend Kate, here."

Kate cocked an eyebrow at Hannah.

"I'll tell you everything after lunch!" Hannah whispered as she stood up from their table.

Hannah and Mazie walked toward Colin. "Ah, Mazie," Colin's face brightened. He reached into his pocket and pulled out a treat. Hannah was impressed, despite herself, with his thoughtfulness. The three of them walked out of the lobby and down the street to Cafe Al Fresco. Hannah noted that Mazie didn't seem bothered by Colin today. *Must be the treats*, she thought. So much for the incorruptible police!

When they stepped inside the quaint Italian eatery it was as if they were transported down an alley in Florence. Fairy lights hung over the old hand-made wooden tables. The server greeted them with a bottle of house red. "Oh, none for me, thanks," Hannah said.

Colin nodded approval for the server to fill his glass. "And for the lady," he added.

Hannah subtly pushed her wine glass to the side and moved her water into its place. After making a show of taking a long sip, she placed it down and got right to business. "We are so appreciative of both your offer and your persistence. I'm afraid we will have to put the sale on hold until the crime scene is resolved."

Colin smiled and took a leisurely sip of his wine. "That's considerate of you, but it won't be necessary. My funds have been released, I'm ready to close." Hannah began to object, but Colin continued. "Priscilla Bryant is going 'up the river' for a long, long time. The more time we take to close the deal, the more potential red tape there may be. I say we close it as soon as possible to avoid getting tangled up in it."

Hannah managed a tight smile. "I understand your position, Mr. Troughton." Colin's eyes held hers at the formal use of his last name. "I just don't think it's completely ethical to proceed at this point."

The server returned with a basket of bread. Colin reached for some and mindlessly ripped off a small piece, reaching under the table to feed Mazie. "I respectfully disagree, Hannah." At his pointed use of her informal first name, she darted her eyes to the side. "Let's move forward, shall we?" he held up his glass as if to ask for a toast.

Hannah lifted her water to her mouth, avoiding the cheers. "Let's give it some time." She was becoming increasingly uncomfortable with his insistence to go ahead with the deal. And his lack of regard for her opinion. "Mr. Troughton," she began, frustration rising. "Might I ask why you are so insistent to close this deal?

Colin placed his wine glass down and sat back in his chair. His arms hung to the side as if to intimidate her with how relaxed he was about this line of questioning.

Hannah mustered up enough courage to continue. "Is there a chance that your eagerness has to do with your desire to tie up loose ends? Might you have something to do with the death of Willard Bryant?" She wiped her sweaty palms on her lap and waited for his response.

Colin was not prepared for her comment. His fists curled at his sides. "Are you telling me that my desire to purchase a house as a developer makes me a suspect in a murder investigation?" His voice got louder with each word.

Hannah held her ground and didn't respond.

"This is preposterous. As far as I'm concerned, the deal is off." He stood up, grabbing his wallet and phone. He took one last piece of bread and tossed it to Mazie, glaring at Hannah the whole time. Mazie nibbled the bread happily, completely unphased by the disagreement that had just taken place.

Hannah watched Colin's muscled back stalk away from her as he neared the restaurant exit. She'd done the right thing. She sighed and glanced down at Mazie. "And you," she muttered. "How effective could you have been on the police force if you can't even smell the guilt coming off Colin in waves. Are pastries all it takes to take you off the trail of justice?"

Hannah waved the server down and handed her a credit card. She settled the bill and gathered her things to leave. For having done the right thing, she was feeling mysteriously unsettled and her bank account would be a little emptier.

CHAPTER EIGHT

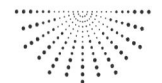

*H*annah walked out of the dim, romantic mood lighting of Cafe Al Fresco into the glare of the afternoon sun. She had to call Kate; she was more suspicious of Colin now than ever. She dialed her number. "Hi Kate, I'm ready to chat. Is now a good time?" The two of them agreed to meet at Jolt of Java. Hannah walked in that direction.

Oscar spotted Hannah and Mazie from behind the counter and met them at the door. He leaned down to scratch behind Mazie's ear before hugging Hannah. Kate was not far behind. Within minutes of Hannah sitting down to her coffee and Mazie munching away at her complimentary croissant, they heard Kate's patrol car door slam to a close. When she sat down, Oscar excused himself back to work behind the counter. Hannah had to physically restrain herself from blurting out all of her worries about Colin as she listened to the updates from Kate.

"We haven't been able to tell if Willard was murdered in the basement, or if his blood got there some other way. We still have strong suspicions that it was Priscilla. We think she overturned his boat. Maybe he died in the basement first and she staged the accident, that's what we're investigating now. You have to admit that Willard leaving his house to her puts her in a high suspicion category. After all, she did have significant business loans outstanding, if you recall."

Hannah murmured as she thought about the validity of the theory. "Then why didn't Priscilla want to sell it at the first chance she got? Even to those who undercut the price, like Megan and Tom?" she asked.

"I can't pretend to know what she was thinking, but her patience did work in her favor," Kate replied. "I suppose an undercut offer is offensive no matter the circumstance."

Hannah sipped her latte and turned her mind back to Colin. He wanted to purchase the land at any cost. Was he going to develop it? Possibly expand his enterprises, or just grow his portfolio? As much as Kate's theory about Priscilla made sense, there were too many questions remaining about Colin. She decided to look into his alibi. If he was nowhere near the area when Willard supposedly drowned, the answer would be clear. On the other hand, if he was in town, that would be a whole other story altogether.

Hannah felt Kate's eyes on her as she mulled it all over.

"Remember, Hannah. Leave the investigation to the professionals. You could get yourself into a lot of trouble if you happen across sensitive information."

Hannah had already decided on her plan of attack but played along. "Yes, I understand." She purposely didn't mention what she had up her sleeve. That way she didn't have to lie about it.

Thankfully, Kate only had time for a quick coffee and was back in her car waving goodbye to Hannah. But it had more of a jerky warning gesture than a casual goodbye motion. Kate's eyes were stern behind the windshield.

Hannah plastered on a big, bright smile, hoping Kate would be distracted by it and stop worrying about her meddling. So that she could get right to meddling. She called her head office. "Jake, hi. It's Hannah. Would you please connect me to Colin Troughton's administrative assistant? I need to get some details from her for our pending deal." There, that all sounded perfectly legitimate. She waited for only a few minutes while Jake flipped through files to find what she was asking for.

"Here it is," he said. "Shall I put you through to her?"

"That would be amazing, thanks," Hannah replied.

The phone rang to Colin's Manhattan offices and Hannah had to switch the phone to her other hand since it was slipping from her sweaty palms. Once more she found herself twirling her hair, waiting, debating whether or not to hang up.

The decision was made for her when her thoughts were interrupted by a cheerful, professional voice. "Colin Troughton's office. How may I help you?"

Though Hannah had been waiting for the phone to stop ringing, it still startled her. She coughed. "Um. Hello." *Fake it till you make it!* She admonished herself. She squared her shoulders and cleared her voice. "Hello, there. This is the traffic department of Blairstown, Virginia. We are trying to verify whether a red-light traffic ticket belongs to a Mr. Colin Troughton. We have a fuzzy picture and I can't read the last number of his license plate." Hannah stopped speaking and held her breath waiting to see if her story would work.

"One moment, I can verify the plate number for you," came the voice.

"Actually," said Hannah, emboldened, "if you could verify whether or not he was in the area on the date in question that would suffice. Let me see, it would have been last Friday." Hannah's face was a bright, tomato red. Guilt-red. She couldn't believe it was working.

"Let me check his calendar." Hannah heard the click of a keyboard over the phone and waited. She looked down at Mazie who had been lounging at her feet but was now sitting proud on her hind legs, alert and watching Hannah. "Blairstown, you said? Last Friday?" clarified Colin's assistant.

"Yes," Hannah all but whispered her response.

"I'm sorry to say that he was indeed there. Feel free to forward the ticket to me and I'll be sure it gets taken care of immediately." His assistant sounded apologetic. Hannah wondered what it would be like to have someone handling even your tickets for you. Great, she imagined.

"We will do just that, thank you kindly for your time," Hannah replied. Then she hung up before she was asked any more questions. "So, Colin was in town. I knew it! I have to tell Kate," she said aloud to Mazie. Hannah turned to tap on the window to ask Oscar and Anita if they would watch Mazie as she went on her next mission. She saw them gathered in a circle with their staff. Darn, they had a staff meeting to run.

Hannah sighed and picked up Mazie's leash. "Now we're heading to do some detective work. That's your profession. I wonder how useful you're going to be?" she directed the question to Mazie as they headed to Colin's hotel. Hannah would confront him and find out for sure. She pushed Kate's voice warning her to leave the investigation to the police out of her mind. She was involved now and she needed that sale, so she had to get to the bottom of this mystery. Well, that was her excuse and she was sticking to it.

CHAPTER NINE

Hannah and Mazie walked from the coffee shop to the hotel in record time. Hannah had a pep in her step and was ready to confront Colin. She waved at the front desk clerk and slid into the elevator that was waiting with open doors in the lobby. She pressed the number twenty-five and together, she and Mazie watched the digital numbers go up. The doors opened; her confidence had increased with each floor they sailed by.

"Let's go, Mazie," Hanna said as they stepped into the hallway. Hannah knew where to go and lead the way. When they reached Colin's room, she confidently knocked on the door three times and waited. She stood so that if he were to look through the peephole, he'd see her clearly. She didn't hear any footsteps or movement, so tried again a little louder this time. Again, nothing. She pressed her ear to the door to see if she could hear a shower running. Nothing. She turned to Mazie and curled her lip in disgust. "How much do you want to bet he skipped town after I started asking him questions?"

Mazie looked up at Hannah and wagged her tail.

"Right. Change of plans then," Hannah said, walking back to the elevator. "We're going to the Bryant house."

Mazie, who was just happy to be along for the ride and close to Hannah, followed along wagging her little tail.

Hannah and Mazie walked along the tree-lined sidewalk back to Priscilla Bryant's house. Hannah was sure Colin would have stopped by the house before he left. He was too excited about the property to leave well-enough alone. Once they arrived, she let herself in with the key in the realtor's box. Unhooking Mazie's leash she carefully walked around the house to look for hints that he'd been there.

Mazie re-familiarized herself with the home by sniffing every corner. It didn't take long for Mazie to find her way to the kitchen where she no doubt smelled leftovers. But instead of focusing her efforts on the refrigerator, or even the pantry, she was back at what Hannah now knew was the basement door. Mazie's sniffing sounded like frantic, sharp inhales.

"That door again, huh? All right, I didn't find anything up here, let's see what's down there." Hannah opened the door and peered down old wooden stairs to the basement. She couldn't see anything in the deep black, so she pulled the string attached to the single lightbulb over the stairs. She was nervous about what she would find and imagined a huge bloodstain after what Kate had said, but she knew she should see the state of the full house as its official realtor.

If it were possible, Mazie's sniffing increased in urgency. Hannah's own nostrils were assaulted with a damp, musty smell that all but overpowered her. She stuck her hand in her sleeve and used it to cover her nose. Slowly, she walked down the stairs with the beagle coming behind her.

The single lightbulb from the stairs highlighted another light switch at the base of them; she flipped it. The florescent lights illuminated an old white freezer against the cement wall, a washing machine, and a dryer, but there didn't seem to be much else. There certainly wasn't the big pool of blood she had been afraid of.

"Not much down here," she said to Mazie. "What was the big fuss?"

At this, Mazie scampered to the corner to a pile of clothes. Or that's what she thought, but then she noticed a leg from beneath the clump of pants move, ever so slightly. She focused her eyes and let them travel to the person's - yes, it was a person - head. She let out a little gasp. "Colin!" she called and ran over to him. He was lying slumped in the corner. His eyes were closed, and he looked lifeless.

Her heart was pounding so hard she feared it might break through her ribs. She had found a body... no... she had seen him move. This gave her enough courage to run over and gently tap his cheeks. "Colin, Colin! Wake up. Are you okay?"

Colin's eyes managed to open with what seemed to be a great effort. She saw his eyeballs rollback.

"Colin! Tell me what happened to you down here!"

Colin closed both eyes tight before trying to open them again. When he did, he looked directly at Hannah, as if focusing on her would will him awake. "I don't know," he slurred.

"Come on, try your best," she verbally pushed him.

With a groan, he placed his hands behind his seat to help reposition himself from being slumped over. Gingerly looking from side to side, he placed his hand on the back of his head and winced. The pain seemed to wake him up. "I had to come by here one more time. I was walking to the back door and felt a blow to the back of my head. It's the last thing I remember. I didn't see or hear anything beforehand."

Hannah stared hard at Colin. As he was knocked out, she had to have been wrong about him. What had she missed? It had to be obvious. Whoever it was, they were territorial about this house. Priscilla was locked up. She was the realtor and she knew it wasn't her. Colin was down in a basement almost unconscious. That left... Megan and Tom! The Weavers had to have done this. But, why? Just so the deal could go to them? If so, Colin wasn't the most competitive one after all. With a chuckle, she thought that was hard to believe.

"Colin, can you stay down here? I'm going to go upstairs and pretend to prepare for another showing. It's the only way I can justify being here, and keep you, well, us, safe. Can you do that for me?" Her eyes were pleading.

He nodded in response, flinching at the pain of the slight movement. "I've not much choice at the moment," he managed.

Mazie placed her front paws on Colin's legs and gave him one big lick. The corner of one of Colin's lips turned up in an attempted smile.

Hannah and Mazie made their way back up the stairs. Hannah's heart was beating in her throat, the adrenaline was pumping through her so hard that her hands were shaking as she grasped the handrail. Taking deep breaths she walked around the house. Tidying this and straightening that. Looking at the house as if she was trying to decide if it was perfect. As she began to straighten the items on the kitchen counter she heard a knock at the front door. Mazie responded by howling and running to the door.

Hannah managed to open it and fake a smile. "Tom and Megan!" she greeted the Weavers, the force from her voice covering the shaking. "Come on in. What brings you back here?"

Tom stepped into the house casually. "We've heard through the rumor mill that the owner is under arrest. We thought that might provide us all an opportunity to revisit our original offer." Tom's chin lifted slightly, and he stared down at Hannah, willing her to shut him down. "We can't imagine Priscilla would have any objections to our offer from behind bars," he added with a big smile that made her want to vomit.

Hanna managed to force a smile and led them to the kitchen. Mazie followed at their feet, tail wagging at the prospect of more people to pet her. "That sounds reasonable to me," she answered. Leaving out the minor detail that a better offer from Colin had already been accepted. "Take a seat, tell me what you had in mind."

Tom jumped at the opportunity. "We love the house. Don't we, Megan?" he asked, looking at his wife.

She nodded and spoke as if his words tagged her to say, *your turn.* "We've looked at dozens of homes, and this is the one we keep thinking about. We realize our last offer was very low, and how that may have offended Priscilla. We're willing to offer you something more."

"Not full asking," Tom jumped in. "But enough to make Priscilla happy. And I'm sure you'll be pleased with your commission," he cocked an eyebrow in Hannah's direction.

Hannah felt a chill go up and down her spine. Mazie noticed and sat up, alert. Hannah had a bad feeling about them, but she had to play along. "I'll, of course, have to run it by Priscilla, even if she's behind bars. But

I'm sure she'll be more than happy to move the house off her plate when she's busy dealing with... well, other things." She darted her eyes up to Tom and Megan who were sharing a sideways-glance. They were obviously pleased.

Mazie had been sitting beside Hannah during the conversation, but she began to sniff the air, then the ground. She found her way to Megan's purse and began to dig her nose in it. Megan didn't notice right away as her purse was under the table, but when she felt Mazie rub against her ankle, she jerked her head to see what it was. When she saw Mazie with her snout all the way in her bag. She shrieked. "Get. Out!" shoving Mazie away with her foot.

Hannah could understand her annoyance, but the physical response shocked her. It brought her back to their first meeting when Megan shoved Mazie away from her that time too. She'd also been digging in her purse at that time.

Hannah jumped to her feet. "Don't kick my dog." At this, Mazie came out from under the table with something in her mouth. A dark look flashed across Tom's face as he realized what it was. Hannah took a moment to register, but when she did, she saw that it was a hammer. With fresh-looking red blood on the head.

Her mind flashed to Colin's blood-stained shirt downstairs and she lost her resolve to play it cool in front of the Weavers. She began to back up in the direction of the front door, chuckling nervously. "Thanks so much for coming by today," her voice rang in a high pitch. "I'll run everything by Priscilla and get back to you as soon as I hear!" She turned to throw the front door open. Tom, realizing what she was about to do lurched at her, tackling her to the ground before she could make an escape. In the scuffle, she'd let go of Mazie's leash. "RUN!" she yelled, hoping the dog would understand. Sure enough, Mazie leaped over the threshold of the doorway and ran like the wind down the steps and onto the sidewalk, the bloodstained hammer gripped in her mouth the whole time.

Tom scrambled to his feet and started after Mazie. He turned to bark at Megan. "Deal with Hannah," and sprinted down the steps. Megan grabbed Hannah's upper arm firmly and jerked her to her feet. Then marched her to the basement door, and down the stairs. There the realtor was once again locking eyes with Colin. Would they end up dead down here? Buried under the floor? Well, at least she'd have company!

CHAPTER TEN

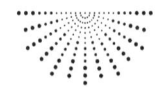

The numbness in Colin's eyes turned to shock when he saw Megan shoving Hannah down the stairs. He was waking up slowly and this was making his eyes slightly more alert than they were before. With Hannah staring at Colin, Megan thrust her into him. "Tie his wrists with this," she said, forcing a chunk of waxy yellow rope in her abdomen.

Hannah looked at the ball of rope, confused. She didn't know how to tie a knot, but she wasn't going to mention that to Megan.

Megan scanned her eyes around the room until she saw something that could function as a weapon. She side-stepped over to grab a piece of 2x2 wood and gripped it watching Hannah with hawk-eyes.

"Turn around," she growled when Hannah was finished. She slid the piece of wood under her armpit and forcefully tied Hannah's wrists behind her back. It seemed as though Megan was more skilled at knot-tying than Hannah had been. Her wrists began to throb immediately.

As Megan tied her, Hannah was thinking a mile a minute. Megan spun her back around, so they were facing one another, Megan once again gripping the wood.

"There's no way you'll get away with this," Hannah tried. "Your best bet is to let us go, we all pretend this never happened and we go back upstairs to talk out our options."

A maniacal laugh escaped from Megan. "Oh, quite the contrary. You see, once Tom returns with Mazie, we'll make it look like Colin killed you and your precious little mutt," she drew her face close to Hannah in a sneer.

Hannah regretted ever referring to Mazie as a mutt.

"Once you two are out of the way, Priscilla will be in the clear, and we'll resume — and succeed, I might add — in negotiating this house from her. Everything is falling into place."

A cold fear sat in the pit of Hannah's stomach. She hated to admit it, but their sinister plan could actually work. "Just one thing," she said. "Why are you and Tom taking such abominable steps for a house?"

Megan's face turned hard. "You didn't meet Willard?"

Hannah shook her head no.

"About ten years ago, Willard and I were neck and neck in negotiations for another development deal. I thought I was going to win the account, but at the last minute he made up a lie about me, and the owner sold to Willard. I was left penniless. I'd given everything I had to secure that deal. So, for ten years, all I've been able to think about is exacting my revenge on him."

"But he's dead?" Hannah said the fact as a question as if to ask what revenge had to do with a dead man's house.

"And for good reason," Megan responded with an evil glint in her eye. "You can imagine that I'd been keeping tight tabs on Willard over the years. When I learned that this house was a family property, Tom and I conspired to capsize Willard's boat, then bury his body in a shallow, unmarked grave. With him out of the picture, it would be easy enough for Tom and me to scoop in and undercut the value of the home, taking my ultimate revenge."

Realization sank into Hannah as she acknowledged what a cold-hearted killer was standing in front of her. Her eyes widened. Megan, relishing the audience continued on. "When Priscilla proved a hard nut to crack, Tom and I made the decision to frame her for Willard's death. We needed her out of the way to buy the home. But since I'm nothing, if not flexible, Colin's presence here will work for that same purpose. She looked over at Colin in disgust. Then back to Hannah. "And you, my dear, you'll just end up as collateral damage. My apologies for that. You seem..." she looked up and down the length of Hannah's body, "nice."

Hannah had been listening carefully and was ready to discuss the flaws in Megan's plan. "What about the fact that Colin offered more than you did? That doesn't seem to fit the profile of someone who'd have to murder to get the home?"

Megan hadn't known this information, her head jerked to look at Colin. Meanwhile, Colin had been trying to break free from the loose knot Hannah had tied around his wrist and was attempting to rise to his feet. Megan acted on instinct and bashed him over the shoulder with the wood plank. An already dazed and weak Colin sank back to the floor. She turned to Hannah with wild eyes, ready to strike her down when the urgent sound of sirens pierced through the basement.

Megan looked desperate. She climbed on an old crate to get a view out of the basement window.

Three police cruisers screeched to a halt in front of the Bryant home. She spotted Tom handcuffed in the back seat of one of the cars. Mazie was in the front seat, barking furiously. Megan slumped down and scanned the damp basement once again. This time not looking for a weapon, but an escape. Looking up, she saw a string hanging from a pull ladder. "Storm door!" she muttered to herself. She began to scamper over to it when Hannah charged forward.

Hannah's own life had just been threatened by this admitted murderer. She was not letting her get away. She lurched her body forward, wrists still secure behind her back, and head-butted Megan with such force, it threw them both away from each other on impact. The women both screamed at the pain. A dazed Megan took a moment to gather herself and ran for Hannah. Hannah was still standing but only just. Megan dove for her feet, kicking them out from under her and hoping to buy time to climb the ladder and escape out of the storm door.

Hannah's body hit the floor with a tremendous bang, and she groaned. Megan took her opportunity and turned to run. Before she could take three steps toward the ladder, a familiar barking came charging down the stairs.

"Mazie!" Hannah cried.

Mazie wasted no time at all, she growled at Megan, backing her into a corner on the other side of the ladder. Then Mazie began to gnaw at the rope tying Hannah's wrists. The sharp little teeth worked their magic in no time, and soon Hannah was free. She used her newly liberated hands to push herself off the ground and leap toward Megan. She held her down with a knee on her back until she couldn't wiggle free.

Though it felt like forever, a short while later, Kate and three other officers descended the stairs and immediately apprehended Megan.

"You'll be joining your husband in jail, ma'am," Kate said to Megan. "One of my officers saw a beagle running in front of Jolt of Java with a hammer in its mouth. As if that weren't strange enough, there was a man who'd been in hot pursuit of the dog trying to wrestle a hammer out of its mouth. And if that weren't the worst of it, the hammer was splattered with blood, which we've already been able to ascertain belonged to none other than Willard Bryant."

Megan sprang to her own defense. "Officer, you have it all wrong! My husband, Tom, duped me into being a part of this. I had no idea anyone had died. I was just trying to buy a home with him!"

Hannah jumped in. "Kate, do not listen to her. She was the ringleader of this whole operation. She carried a vendetta against Willard and planned how to kill him and seek revenge by buying and destroying his house!"

Kate looked confused and Hannah understood. Kate loved her, but the last time they spoke, she was trying to convince her that Colin — the man slumped over and tied up in the corner — was the murderer. On the other hand, it was unlikely Megan didn't know anything about the murder when her husband carried a bloody hammer.

Colin had been quiet the whole time, but he was suddenly making a commotion in the corner. He was trying to move his body to reach his phone. When he did, he shoved it over to Hannah. She reached down to pick it up and saw the Voice Recorder app was blinking.

"You recorded our whole conversation?" she asked, flabbergasted.

"Full confession," Colin managed to eke out in a weak voice.

Kate pressed play and listened to the full conspiracy echoed back to her. She turned to Megan. "You are under arrest, little madam."

Megan somehow managed to find ways to protest her arrest all the way to the cruiser, kicking and screaming up the stairs.

Hannah felt her adrenaline plummet once Megan was gone. The remaining police officers began to mark areas off with yellow tape to collect evidence from the basement. And the paramedics were helping Colin onto a stretcher.

"Wow!" was all Hannah could think to say. She reached down to pat Mazie on the head. "Looks like you came through for me in the end, little buddy. And in a big way. Thanks," she whispered and kissed Mazie on the nose.

She turned her attention to Colin, who'd been watching the whole exchange. He flashed a tired, but still dazzling smile at her before he was taken up the stairs to the ambulance.

CHAPTER ELEVEN

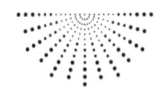

One week later, Hannah was sitting in Jolt of Java, chatting with Anita and Oscar over a steaming cup of coffee. Mazie had graduated from the outdoor tables to a spot indoors, right next to the fireplace. Complete with her own dog bed.

"It's the least we can do for our canine hero," Anita said. "I even saw Oscar searching for "plaques" on his phone one morning."

They were mid-conversation about potential new seasonal coffee offerings when Hannah's phone buzzed on the table. They all caught sight of the contact that lit up; Priscilla Bryant.

Anita politely averted her eyes, while Oscar blatantly said, "Good luck with that!" and crossed his arms over his chest, leaning back in his seat and watching her, as if getting ready to enjoy the show.

"Hi, Mrs. Bryant," Hannah began. She listened politely to the woman speaking. "Yes, congratulations on your freedom!" she responded.

Oscar leaned forward in his chair to try and listen.

"Of course. I understand why you'd feel that way. Why don't you come to the Jolt of Java? I'm already here, so any time works for me. Great, see you then." Hannah hung up the phone and gave an update to her curious tablemates. "She'll be here in ten minutes."

Oscar and Anita were careful to busy themselves for Priscilla's arrival. When she arrived exactly ten minutes later, she carried with her a familiar energy, but it felt like the edge had been taken off slightly. Her makeup was muted, her hair softer. Jeans had replaced her standard pencil skirt, but she still wore her signature silk blouse.

Hannah stood to greet her. Priscilla spotted her and though she didn't volunteer an embrace, she offered a squeak of a smile before sitting. "Right," she began. "Let's get to business."

Hannah stifled a laugh. I guess prison hadn't taken the edge completely off.

"I'm obviously very grateful to be vindicated, which says nothing about the fact that I was wrongly apprehended in the first place." She folded her hands on the table in front of her. "I want the house sold. The cost is no longer an issue for me. Whoever offers the first decent amount gets the place. I just want it gone."

Hannah could sense the meeting was over. She smiled and reached her hand out for a shake. "Consider it done. I'll get to work on it right away. In fact, I think I may just know someone."

Priscilla stood, shook Hannah's hand, and was out the door as efficiently as she came in.

Hannah knew exactly where to start. She hadn't seen Colin since the day he had been taken away in the ambulance, but she thought a week would be sufficient time for him to feel up to visitors. She waved goodbye to Anita and Oscar and lead Mazie out the door to a flower shop. After getting a bouquet of fresh-cut stems, she walked to his hotel. She and Mazie took the elevator up to the twenty-fifth floor. The door opened with a ding and Mazie seemed to lead the way to Colin's door. Hannah knocked gently.

She heard a shuffling movement behind the door and a snap as the door unlocked. Colin opened the door. He stood there in jeans and a t-shirt. His tall frame filling both out in a way that surprised Hannah. Somehow, she was expecting someone sicklier.

"Hannah," he greeted her with a gentle smile. "Nice to see you again, come on in."

Mazie's tail began waving back and forth when she heard Colin's voice and she sat at his feet, waiting for him to pet her.

"Ah, Mazie — our hero!" he said, lowering to pat her head.

Hannah handed him the flowers. "It's not much, but I do hope you're feeling better," she offered.

He opened the door wider and gestured for them to head to the sitting area in his expansive room.

Hannah sat on the single chair, leaving the comfortable velvet couch strewn with various Band-Aids and ointments for Colin. Mazie hopped up on the couch beside him, resting her chin on his thigh. Colin smiled and placed his hand on her back.

"How are you feeling?" Hannah asked.

"You know, I've certainly been better. But I have to say the recovery is going faster than I anticipated. I expect to head back to Manhattan tomorrow morning," he replied.

"That makes me happy to hear," Hannah grinned. "And it might leave just the right amount of time for this offer," she pulled out a folder filled with papers from her bag. "Priscilla Bryant is ready to close. What do you say?"

Colin straightened his spine an inch. "Hmmm," he paused. "You know, given my history with the place, I'm not sure it would be a wise business deal for me. There may be too many emotions for me to treat it professionally."

Hannah nodded in understanding. "I had a feeling, but I wanted you to have the first right of refusal."

"And I appreciate that," he said, looking right into her eyes. He crossed his right ankle over his left knee and sat back on the couch, grateful that was out of the way.

"If you want to forget about Blairstown entirely, I'd understand. However, I do have a few other houses in mind that may be of interest to you?" she tossed the offer out gently, seeing if it would stick.

Colin responded with his signature beam of a smile. "I'd like that very much." Then he shifted slightly in his seat. "Hannah. I haven't yet thanked you for saving my life. I'm not sure how things for me would have ended that day had you," then he scratched Mazie's ear, "and Mazie not been there." He rested his eyes meaningfully on Hannah's.

Hannah grinned in return. Her fingers involuntarily began twirling her blonde hair. "I'd love to continue working with you. I'll send those other properties to your office for your review."

Colin tried in vain to suppress a yawn.

"I'll leave you to your recovery," Hannah said, standing up. "You'll let me know if you need anything, I hope?" she asked.

Colin nodded. "You'll forgive me for not walking you to the door?" he asked, pointing to his head.

"Of course!" Hannah walked to the door, Mazie hopped off the couch and followed behind her. When Hannah got to the door, she turned back to Colin. "All the best to you and your recovery." Then she and Mazie slipped out.

With a slight flush, Hannah and Mazie headed down to the street level for a little walk. They could both use it to burn off some energy. Mazie pulled the leash slightly so she could sniff something in the bushes. Hannah looked down at the pup and found that she had a warmth spreading through her body. Her feelings toward Mazie had shifted; she was no longer bothered by the dog's curiosity, the warmth inside was admiration.

"Let's get you a special treat later today. Maybe a croissant?" she asked the dog. Mazie continued sniffing, oblivious to the suggestion. They continued on their stroll when Hannah heard a voice call her name.

She turned to see the source. She spotted a mop of curly blond hair atop a tall, athletic frame. "NILES!" she called. Mazie seemed to recognize the name and abruptly stopped sniffing. She brought her head up to the direction Hannah was calling and sniffed the air. Mazie was off in a sprint, Hannah behind her, running all the way to reunite with Niles.

CHAPTER TWELVE

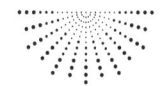

Hannah fell into the comfort of Niles' embrace. She gripped him a little bit tighter than usual, it was so nice to be in the safety and comfort of her cousin's presence.

Niles chuckled and patted her back. "Nice to see you too, Cuz," he let her linger as long as she needed. Meanwhile, Mazie was barking and jumping up and down, waiting for her turn. When Hannah let go, Niles happily got down to the ground and let Mazie jump and lick him all over. He laughed. "I'm pretty sure they didn't teach you this in the police academy, but I don't mind," he smiled as Mazie licked every inch of his face.

Niles placed his arm around Hannah's shoulder, took the leash from her and they continued on their walk.

"Seems like I may have missed a few stories while I was away."

Hannah relaxed into his shoulder. She looked up at the gorgeous colors on the fall trees. They seemed even richer than they had when Niles was last here. She breathed in the earthy air and sighed.

"I can't thank you enough for watching Mazie while I was gone. I hope she wasn't too much trouble," he said.

Hannah let her eyes fall to the boundless energy of fur walking slightly ahead of them. "No trouble at all," she said.

"But I don't want you to worry, I've got a few leads on another foster family for her," continued Niles.

Hannah stiffened slightly. She hadn't anticipated Mazie would be gone so soon. She felt like she and Mazie had just begun to settle into a routine. The thought of Mazie leaving filled her with an unexpected emptiness. "Well, Niles. This is probably going to come as much as a surprise to you as it has to me, but..." Hannah paused for dramatic effect, "I'd like Mazie to stay with me. Indefinitely."

At this announcement, Niles pulled his arm off of Hannah's shoulder. He brought his hands to his hips and stopped abruptly. He stared at her as if she was a mirage. He finally found his words. "I guess shocked is an understatement," he replied. The two of them continued walking. "What did this little furball do to wiggle her way into your heart so fast?" he asked.

"That's a long story," Hannah said slyly. She looked up and saw a familiar figure on the sidewalk ahead. She'd recognize that chestnut bob anywhere. "Kate!" Hannah yelled. The figure kept walking. "Kate Carver!" she tried again. At this, Kate's slim figure turned to face Hannah's voice.

"Hannah!" she replied, raising her hand in a slight wave. She walked toward them. When she arrived, she greeted Mazie with a friendly pat. "Catch any new murder suspects since I last saw you?"

Niles's eyes went wide and his head turned to Hannah. Her reaction would determine if that was a joke or something he needed to be concerned about.

Hannah laughed and glanced at Niles. She shrugged as if to communicate, *what can I say?*

Niles extended his hand to Kate. "I'm Niles French, police officer." He glanced at Kate's badge and tried for a joke. "I'd like to ask you a few questions."

Kate appreciated the humor and laughed generously. "I'll try to summarize," and she launched into a high-level overview of last week's events.

"Ahh," said Niles when Kate wrapped up. "First of all, I'm impressed. Well done on your detective work, Cuz," he patted her back. "And I understand your connection to Mazie now. Looks like she found her loving home, and you found your new partner in crime," Niles' easy smile fell over them all.

Kate looked up at Niles. "What do you say you and I grab a drink and I retell that story in police-level detail?" she offered.

Niles's shoulders lifted. "Police-level detail is one of my favorite pastimes!" he replied. Niles handed the leash back to Hannah. "I'll swing by your place later tonight."

"Dinner?" offered Hannah.

"You bet," he replied. Then he left with Kate to swap law enforcement stories.

Hannah and Mazie were left together again. Hannah crouched down to nuzzle Mazie's snout. "You probably realized pretty soon that I wasn't in the market for a pet."

Mazie responded by sneaking a lick up Hannah's cheek. "But you've proven to be more than just a pet," she continued, "you're a true partner. And I can't believe I'm saying this, but I'm willing to put my complete trust in you."

Mazie's tail wagged enthusiastically. By now, Hannah knew Mazie couldn't understand the words, but she could feel the love. "And don't tell Niles he was right about this, but we really do make a great team."

Hannah looked up to the crisp, blue sky. "Look at that," she said to Mazie. "That sky is so bright and beautiful. It's as if it's showing off, just for us." Hannah and Mazie continued on their walk together, happily heading to Jolt of Java.

"As promised," Hannah handed bits of a croissant to Mazie. "Your well-deserved treat." Mazie gobbled the pastry and sat contentedly beside Hannah, leaning into her leg.

Hannah smiled, thinking back to their eventful escapades together, and how Mazie's instincts had always been right. *I wonder what adventures we have ahead of us?* she thought, scratching behind Mazie's ears.

* * *

If you enjoyed this book, you can grab the complete Dog Detective – The Beagle Mysteries here

DOG DETECTIVE – A BULLDOG ON THE CASE BOOKS 1 TO 6 – PREVIEW

The voice in her head was childlike and more like a thought than an actual voice but it helped. Whether it was real or just in her imagination it didn't matter.

"Be calm, let go. I here, I help, all okay."

It was bad enough that the steering wheel was on the wrong side but now she had to cope with this. Lola Ramsey leaned her head on the wheel and took a long deep breath. The pain was like someone kneeling on her chest and she gasped for every lungful of air as if her life depended on it. With shaking hands and sweat running down her back she felt herself back in the heat of the dessert.

Reaching over to the left, she rubbed the soft fur between the Frenchie's ears and felt herself start to relax. The next breath came easier and her throat seemed to open. The shaking eased up too and she relaxed her grip on the steering wheel. Letting the breath out, she took another and felt the dizziness pass too. It was replaced with a touch of anger. Logically, she knew that the bang had just been a car backfiring. Logically, she knew there was no danger and most of the time now, you wouldn't know about her severe case of PTSD. But then, just when she thought she had it under control, something like this happened.

Annoyance replaced her fear and she sat up and brushed a lock of black hair from her face. It had escaped the bun she wore and sweat had stuck it to her lip. A picture formed in her mind of Smokey and the Bandit though she doubted her thin hair would give her quite such a fabulous mustache. Did that picture come from Sassy or from her own mind? It didn't matter, it broke her from her fear.

Wiping the sweat away she stared out of the window. The black bonnet of the Discovery Sport was not exactly parked as straight as she would have liked, but at least she had pulled to the right, well left-hand sidewalk, curb – she must try and get the language right.

This attack had been a bad one... her first in months. Though she could've kept driving, the last thing she wanted to do was meet her friend in such a panic. So, in desperation, she'd thrown the car over to the sidewalk and killed the engine.

As her breathing returned to normal she was aware that sweat was dripping down her back and off her forehead but the shake in her knees and hands was almost gone.

"You okay?" the thought was back in her head and a feeling of love and warmth came with it.

Lola smiled. "Thanks, and I'm good now," she said to the little French Bulldog strapped to the seatbelt in the seat next to her. She could have sworn that the little dog smiled and once more she felt the feeling of love.

At one time, this strange communication she had with animals had terrified her. Lola had been in the military and was serving in Afghanistan when her unit stumbled on an IED. Many of her friends perished that day. The memory brought with it its own pain but she pushed it down. It was not her fault, surviving was not her fault either. While others had died, she had been thrown clear by the blast. When she landed her head hit a rock and even with her helmet, the force, increased by the explosion, was enough to cause a severe head injury. There had been temporal and occipital lobe damage according to her doctors.

Though she was now completely recovered, except for the PTSD, she had developed this ability to communicate with animals. At first, it had scared her and she had been terrified of letting anyone know. They would all think she was crazy and the last thing she wanted was to be locked up.

Luckily, she had been befriended by a baker called Melody Hennessey and her cute and intelligent French Bulldog, Smudge. Between them, Melody and Smudge had taught her to accept this as a gift. Melody had told her that even if it was all in her mind, what did it matter? It was hurting no one and the things that Lola heard were remarkably similar to what Melody thought that Smudge would be saying. They posited that it was either a true gift or that Lola's subconscious was reading the dog's body language and making up this voice to match what it saw. Either way, it had proved very useful.

With the help of Melody and Smudge, and a couple of murder mysteries, Lola had recovered her sense of who she was. Then one day, she found herself at the local pound and there was this frightened and skinny little French Bulldog puppy with the most beautiful coat and eyes she had ever seen. Courtney, who ran the shelter, told her that the color was called Isabella or lilac. It was actually a pale grayish brown but it really did look lilac and the dog's eyes were the most stunning amber. They pulled you in and you just wanted to stare at them and be entranced by their beauty. They were as pretty as amber rocks and seemed to hold a deep and intuitive intelligence.

The puppy was very scared and little was known about her background except that she had been dumped. Though Courtney had shown her the puppy, she hadn't intended for her to adopt her. Lola had never had a dog before and this one was going to need a lot of care to get her to trust people. Of course, Courtney didn't know about Lola's special ability.

The minute she locked eyes with the puppy, she had instantly been able to communicate with the dog and before long the two of them were the best of friends. When she asked the little dog what she would like as a name, the little pup told her that a nice lady once called her Sassy Pants and gave her a cookie; she liked it so much that she called herself that to remind herself of the good time. Lola had chuckled at the name but had been saddened that one cookie was the little pup's idea of a good time. Still, Sassy it was.

At the time, Lola had been staying with a fellow veteran, Jake, in Port Warren, New Jersey, USA. She loved it there but she also knew that she had to start again and make a life for herself.

When it was time for her to move on, Jake had managed to get her and the puppy enrolled at a center where they trained therapy dogs. Sassy had passed with flying colors and was now her official therapy dog. The center and Jake had encouraged Lola to go back to her old life. Lola didn't know where to begin but just at that time she had received a call from an old friend from England. They had been to college together. That was why, after a long flight, she was now driving down a quiet road surrounded by grazing cattle on her way to South-Brooke, Lincolnshire, England.

They were just five minutes away from her friend, Tanya Buchanan's house and the panic attack had taken her by surprise. Tanya was an art teacher and had invited Lola to stay with her until she could find a place of her own. Though part of her was really looking forward to this, another part of her was terrified. Was that what had caused the panic attack? Had her own fear of the future brought her back to the past?! Her fear of stepping out and living life again, her fear of seeing people hurt?

"Breathe," the voice said inside her head.

Lola nodded and took in a deep breath, letting it calm her and lower her heart rate. Letting it out, she took another and after the third one, she started to feel better. There were still worries and questions but with Sassy at her side, she would deal with them.

"Bird, birds, birds, birds... let me out, have to chase," Sassy said. The voice was now high-pitched, almost a scream, and the little dog's whole body was tense as she stared out of the side window at a sparrow.

The small brown bird hopped along a beautiful almost molded green hedge. It was minding its own business and had no idea how close the almost rabid Frenchie was.

Lola chuckled, Sassy could be serious and comforting one moment and intent on ridding the world of birds in the next. Luckily, she never managed to catch any.

Lola stroked her once more and then thought about this move. How would she cope with this new start? Would the panic attacks stop her from moving forward? And, what would she do with her life?

That was the big question.

Though her military career was over, with her trust fund she had more than enough money to never need to work again, but she couldn't imagine not being productive for the rest of her life. After all, she was only 35. Then there was the fact that she didn't touch her trust fund, even though Melody had tried to persuade her to do so. Melody had told her that there was no harm or shame in it.

Lola took another breath to keep her mind here in the present. It still didn't seem right, not yet. So, here she was trying to decide what to do with her life and wondering if she really could cope.

Putting the Discovery into gear she pulled onto the road. They would soon be at Tanya's. Lola was both dreading and looking forward to seeing her friend again and she knew that Sassy was ready for a walk and something to eat.

"Not long, Pooch," she said.

There were no words in her mind in return just a feeling of excitement that lasted for the rest of the journey.

You can now grab the first 6 Bulldog on the Case books in one great value box set and also FREE with Kindle Unlimited

DOG DETECTIVE – A BULLDOG ON THE CASE BOOKS 1 TO 6 – ...

ALSO BY ROSIE SAMS

Grab free short stories and be the first to find out when Rosie has a new release by joining her free newsletter

* * *

You can now grab the first 6 Bulldog on the Case books in one great value box set and also FREE with Kindle Unlimited

Follow Rosie on BookBub – go here and click the red follow button

Follow Rosie on Amazon – go here click the yellow follow button

If you enjoyed this book, Rosie and Lila would appreciate it if you left a review on Amazon or Goodreads.

©Copyright 2022 Rosie Sams
All Rights Reserved
Rosie Sams

License Notes
This Book is licensed for personal enjoyment only. It may not be resold. Your continued respect for author's rights is appreciated.

This story is a work of fiction; any resemblance to people is purely coincidence. All places, names, events, businesses, etc. are used in a fictional manner. All characters are from the imagination of the author.